This book belongs to

....

BAINTE DEN STOC

WITHDRAWN FROM
DÚN LAOGHAIRE-RATHDOWN CO.
LIBRARY STOCK

DÚN LAOGHAIRE-
RATHDOWN LIBRARIES

DLR27000017839	
BERTRAMS	10/08/2018
GD	02346960

Quarto is the authority on a wide range of topics.

Quarto educates, entertains and enriches the lives of our readers—enthusiasts and lovers of hands-on living.

www.quartoknows.com

© 2018 Quarto Publishing plc

First published in 2018 by QED Publishing,
an imprint of The Quarto Group.
The Old Brewery, 6 Blundell Street,
London N7 9BH, United Kingdom.
T (0)20 7700 6700 F (0)20 7700 8066
www.QuartoKnows.com

All rights reserved. No part of this publication may be reproduced, stored in a retrieval system, or transmitted in any form or by any means, electronic, mechanical, photocopying, recording, or otherwise, without the prior permission of the publisher, nor be otherwise circulated in any form of binding or cover other than that in which it is published and without a similar condition being imposed on the subsequent purchaser.

A catalogue record for this book is available from the British Library.

ISBN 978-1-91241-388-1

Based on the original story by Heidi and Daniel Howarth
Author of adapted text: Katie Woolley
Series Editor: Joyce Bentley
Series Designer: Sarah Peden

Manufactured in Dongguan, China TL042018

9 8 7 6 5 4 3 2 1

MIX
Paper from responsible sources
FSC® C104723
www.fsc.org

Reading
Gems

The Mouse
and the
Lighthouse

QED

Max was a little mouse.
He loved the big blue sea.

Max lived in a lighthouse and helped the keeper look after it.

Max was a happy little mouse.

One day, the lighthouse was very quiet.
Where was the lighthouse keeper?

Max found a letter.
It said 'gone to the dentist'.

But Max was a little mouse.
He could not read.

Max went up to his room.
A puffin was tap, tap,
tapping on the window.

"Hello," said the puffin.

"Hello," said Max.

He was happy to have a friend to chat to.

But where was the lighthouse keeper?

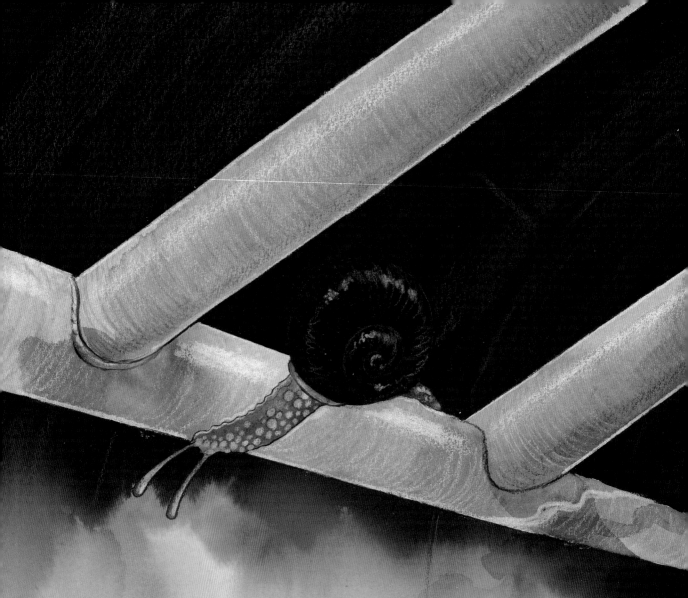

Max had work to do. He had to climb
all the way up to the top of the lighthouse.

He had never done this on his own before.

It was a long way up.

Max slipped
and he fell...

Down, down, down he tumbled.
When he came to a stop, Max saw
he was on a web. There was a big
spider smiling at him.

"My web caught you," the spider said.

Max and the spider climbed all the way to the top of the lighthouse. It was nice to have a friend to chat to.

It had got dark and the light wasn't on. Max could hear a ship's horn.

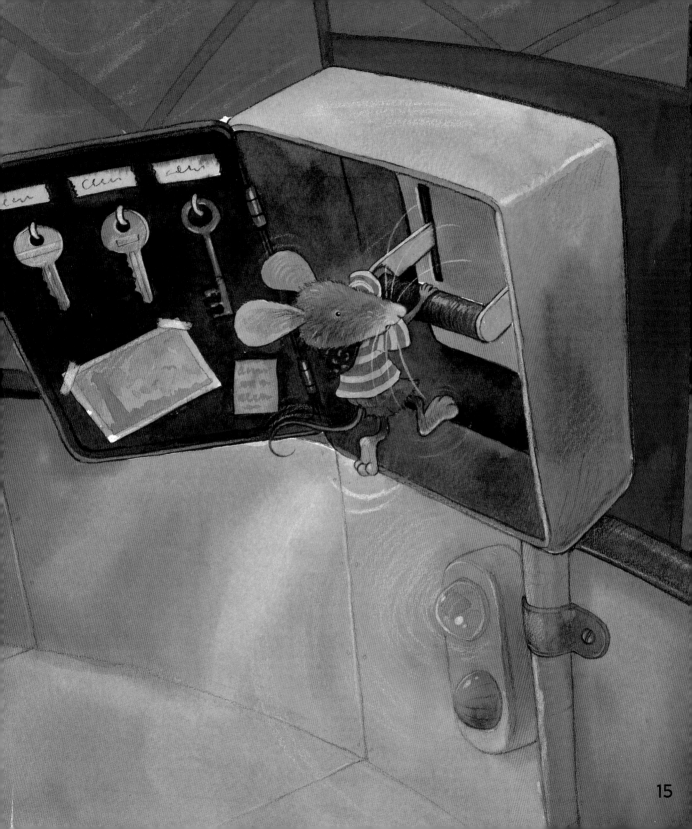

Max needed to fix the light. He needed to get a new light bulb. But it was all the way down at the bottom of the lighthouse.

Then, Max saw his new friends.

"We can help!" they said.

Max and the spider flew down and back up again on the puffin's back.

At the top of the lighthouse, Max got to work. He had soon fixed the light, with the help of his friends.

The bright light lit up the sea. Max could see the ship. It sailed safely away from the rocks below.

"We did it," he said.

Max could sleep well tonight.
He had done a good job.

"Hello, Max," said a voice. It was the lighthouse keeper! Max was glad to see his friend.

He had his old friend back. And now he had
some new friends, too.

Max was a happy little mouse.

Story Words

climb

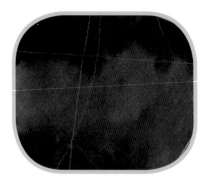

dark

light

light bulb

lighthouse keeper

Max

puffin

read

rocks

24

sea

ship

spider

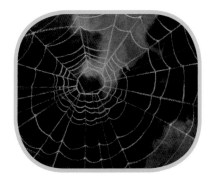

web

window

25

Let's Talk About
The Mouse and the Lighthouse

**Look carefully
at the book cover.**

Could you have guessed
what the story was
about from the cover?

What clues are there?

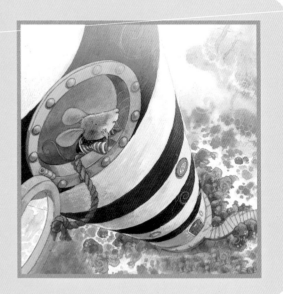

**The story is all about
being a lighthouse keeper.**

What does a lighthouse
keeper do?

Max helps look after the
lighthouse but who looks
after Max when he needs
help to fix the light bulb?

A lighthouse keeper keeps people safe at sea.

What other jobs can you think of that grown ups do to keep others safe?

What job would you like to do when you grow up?

Max learns that it is good to have friends to help you when you need it.

Can you think of any examples of when working together, you can get things done more easily?

Did you like the ending of the story?

What do you think happened next?

Fun and Games

Look back through the story and
put these characters and objects
in the order they appear.

ship

puffin

spider

mouse

letter

lighthouse
keeper

Answers: 1: mouse; 2: letter; 3: puffin; 4: spider; 5: ship; 6: lighthouse keeper.

Look at the pictures and say the words.
Look back through the story and find
sentences that use the words.

light bulb

ship

sea

web

Your Turn

Now that you have read the story,
have a go at telling it in your own words.
Use the pictures below to help you.

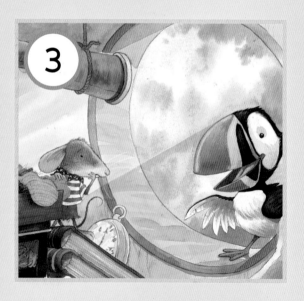

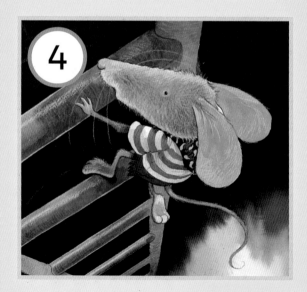

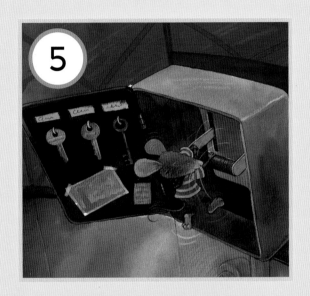

GET TO KNOW READING GEMS

Reading Gems is a series of books that has been written for children who are learning to read. The books have been created in consultation with a literacy specialist.

The books fit into four levels, with each level getting more challenging as a child's confidence and reading ability grows. The simple text and fun illustrations provide gradual, structured practice of reading. Most importantly, these books are good stories that are fun to read!

Level 1 is for children who are taking their first steps into reading. Story themes and subjects are familiar to young children, and there is lots of repetition to build reading confidence.

Level 2 is for children who have taken their first reading steps and are becoming readers. Story themes are still familiar but sentences are a bit longer, as children begin to tackle more challenging vocabulary.

Level 3 is for children who are developing as readers. Stories and subjects are varied, and more descriptive words are introduced.

Level 4 is for readers who are rapidly growing in reading confidence and independence. There is less repetition on the page, broader themes are explored and plot lines straddle multiple pages.

The Mouse and the Lighthouse is all about a little mouse who can do big things with the help of his friends. It looks at the theme of friendship.

Level 3

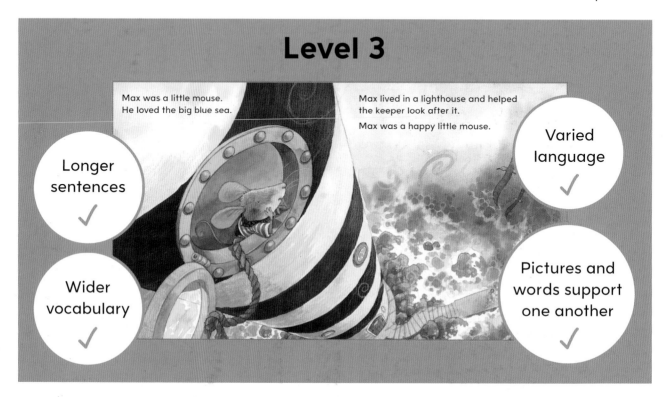

Max was a little mouse. He loved the big blue sea.

Max lived in a lighthouse and helped the keeper look after it.

Max was a happy little mouse.

Longer sentences ✓

Wider vocabulary ✓

Varied language ✓

Pictures and words support one another ✓